CooL COMICS

Creating Fun *and* Fascinating Collections!

ABDO
Publishing Company

Visit us at
www.abdopublishing.com

Published by ABDO Publishing Company, 4940 Viking Drive, Edina, Minnesota 55435.
Copyright © 2007 by Abdo Consulting Group, Inc. International copyrights reserved in all countries.
No part of this book may be reproduced in any form without written permission from the publisher.
The Checkerboard Library™ is a trademark and logo of ABDO Publishing Company.

Printed in the United States.

Design and Production: Mighty Media, Inc.
Cover Photo: Anders Hanson
Interior Photos: Anders Hanson; Shutterstock; All Marvel characters and images are used with permission from Marvel Entertainment, Inc.; Devils Due Publishing; Marvel; The Official Overstreet Comic Book Price Guide, 35th edition, and The Official Overstreet Comic Book Grading Guide, used with permission from Gemstone Publishing; Photo provided by Reed Exhibitions New York Comic Con. Copyright © 2006 Reed Exhibition, a division of Reed Elsevier Inc. All rights reserved; John McCea's original comic art (p. 24), used with permission. Text and illustrations of ArchEnemies™ © 2006 Drew Melbourne. The Goon™ © Eric Powell. Conan® and Conan the Barbarian® (including all prominent characters featured in this issue) and the distinctive likeness thereof are trademarks of Conan Properties International, LLC unless otherwise noted. All contents © Conan Properties International, LLC unless otherwise noted. Published by Dark Horse Comics Inc.

Special thanks: Comic Book College, Nostalgia Zone

Library of Congress Cataloging-in-Publication Data

Price, Pamela S.
   Cool comics / Pam Price.
       p. cm. -- (Cool collections)
   Includes index.
   ISBN-13: 978-1-59679-769-7
   ISBN-10: 1-59679-769-X
  1. Comic books, strips, etc.--United States--History and criticism--Juvenile literature. 2. Comic books, strips, etc.--Collectors and collecting--Juvenile literature. I. Title. II. Series: Cool collections (Edina, Minn.)

PN6725.P75 2007
741.5'97309--dc22   2006011962

Contents

The History of Comic Books

FOR COMIC BOOK COLLECTORS, 1938 WAS AN IMPORTANT YEAR.
That's when Action Comics #1 was published. This is the comic in which the first major superhero, Superman, appeared. But comics existed long before then.

In 1646, the first American cartoon was published. Many early cartoons were like illustrations. They didn't have words or tell a story. The first comic strip with words and a **sequential** story was *The Yellow Kid*. It was published in 1895.

Over time, collections of comic strips were gathered and published. This began what is now called the Platinum Age of comic books. The Platinum Age lasted until the mid-1930s.

The Golden Age of comic books lasted from the mid-1930s through the mid-1950s. This is when comic books as we know them today were first published. This is also when many of the modern superheroes first appeared. **World War II** took place during this time, so many of the early storylines focused on the war.

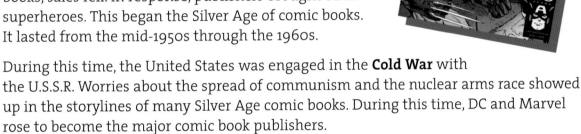

After the war ended, storylines in comic books shifted to crime and horror. Many people were concerned about the content of comic books. The U.S. Senate even held hearings about the content of comic books.

As parents became more upset with the content of comic books, sales fell. In response, publishers brought back superheroes. This began the Silver Age of comic books. It lasted from the mid-1950s through the 1960s.

During this time, the United States was engaged in the **Cold War** with the U.S.S.R. Worries about the spread of communism and the nuclear arms race showed up in the storylines of many Silver Age comic books. During this time, DC and Marvel rose to become the major comic book publishers.

The Bronze Age of comic books spans the 1970s. Comic books continued to mirror current events. The civil and social unrest of the 1970s played a part in the stories. This was also a time of great change in comic book style. New writers and artists reshaped the look and content of comic books.

The modern age of comic books began around 1980 and continues today. Although sales of current comic books rise and fall, classic comic books remain in high demand. In most comic book stores today, you will find collectors of all ages looking for both new and old comic books.

Why Collect?

IT'S IMPORTANT TO UNDERSTAND WHY YOU WANT TO COLLECT COMIC BOOKS. First off, don't think that collecting comic books will make you rich. One reason people pay so much for Golden and Silver Age comic books is their scarcity.

Back then, far fewer copies were printed of each comic book. Most kids treated them badly. They rolled them up and stuck them in their pockets. They wrote on them. They threw them away.

At that time, comic books were printed on newsprint. This cheap paper had a very high acid content. As a result, the comic books yellowed and became very brittle. For all of these reasons, old comic books in excellent condition are expensive today.

Today, there are many more comic book titles being published. Publishers print more copies of each issue. And more people save them, hoping they will be valuable some day.

But it's almost impossible to know today which comic books will appeal to collectors years from now. And, because there are so many copies around, they will probably never be as valuable as the older comic books.

Reasons to Collect Comics

- You enjoy reading them.
- You enjoy learning the history of the comic books.
- You enjoy the process of collecting them.
- You enjoy learning about the artists and writers.
- You enjoy spending time with other collectors.

Deciding What to Collect

COMIC BOOKS FROM THE GOLDEN AGE AND SILVER AGE ARE VERY EXPENSIVE. The people who buy them are adults with plenty of money. Popular Golden Age comics sell for thousands of dollars.

Pricing guides show that Action Comics #1 is valued at about a half-million dollars! Not all older comic books are this expensive. But many desirable comic books cost hundreds if not thousands of dollars.

Narrow Your Focus

Fortunately, not all older comic books are rare or expensive. But, collecting each and every comic book you can afford to buy will get you more of a mess than a collection! When you collect, you need to narrow your focus.

Reading Copies

If you want to collect older comic books, look for what the dealers call reading copies. These are comic books that are fairly common and not in great condition. You can sometimes buy these for a dollar or two.

The storylines in comic books build over the years. It's common to start reading a comic book series and wonder what led to the events in the current storyline. In the world of comic books, this is called story **continuity**. You can catch up by picking up reading copies of back issues.

Publishers also release **anthologies** of Silver Age comics. These books gather many issues in one book. The Marvel Essentials and DC Showcase Presents series are great for continuity. The books are about 500 pages long and are printed in black and white.

Marvel, DC, and Dark Horse also publish color anthologies of Silver Age comic books. These hardcover books are more expensive than the black and white anthologies. But, they are far less expensive than collecting the original comic books.

Story Arcs

A story arc is a shorter story within a series. In comic books, the story arc will usually have its own title within the series. For example, *X-Men: Deadly Genesis* is a six-issue story arc within the X-Men series. One way to build a collection is to collect entire story arcs, new and old.

Collect Writers or Artists

As you read more comics, you will find that some appeal to you more than others. Learn who the artists and writers are, then research what other titles they have worked on. Comic book writers and artists often work for different companies during their careers. Decide whose work you like and collect those comic books.

Writers

These writers are well-known to fans of older and current comic books. Some write individual issues. Others are editors who oversee the storyline and appearance of a series.

Brian Michael Bendis (*Jinx, New Avengers, Ultimate Spider-Man*)

Ed Brubaker (*Captain America, Gotham Central, Sleeper*)

Kurt Busiek (*Astro City, Marvels, Thunderbolts*)

Neil Gaiman (*Death: The High Cost of Living, Sandman, Stardust*)

Mark Millar (*The Authority, The Ultimates, Wolverine*)

Alan Moore (*Swamp Thing, Watch Men, The Killing Joke*)

Grant Morrison (*Animal Man, Invisibles, JLA*)

Denny O'Neil (*Batman, Green Lantern/Green Arrow, The Shadow*)

Brian K. Vaughan (*Runaways, Ultimate X-Men, Y: The Last Man*)

Mark Waid (*Captain America, The Flash, Kingdom Come*)

Joss Whedan (*Astonishing X-Men, Fray, Serenity*)

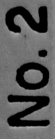

No. 2

Artists

It takes many artists to produce any one comic book. Different artists may sketch, ink, paint, and letter the contents of one comic book. Yet another artist may create the cover art.

Art Adams (*X-Men, Fantastic Four, Monkeyman and O'Brien*)

Neal Adams (*Batman, Green Lantern, Avengers*)

Sergio Aragonés (*Mad Magazine, Groo the Wanderer*)

John Cassaday (*Ghost, Detective Comics, Excaliber*)

Will Eisner (*The Spirit, A Contract with God, The Building*)

Bryan Hitch (*StormWatch, The Authority, Ultimates*)

Phil Jimenez (*Infinite Crisis, New X-Men, Wonder Woman*)

Mike Kaluta (*Fantastic, Starstruck, The Shadow*)

Jack Kirby (*Fantastic Four, Thor, Captain America, The Black Panther*)

Jim Lee (*All Star Batman and Robin, WildC.A.T.s, Infinite Crisis*)

Dave Mazzuchelli (*Daredevil, Batman, Rubber Blanket*)

Frank Miller (*Batman: The Dark Knight Returns, Daredevil, Sin City*)

George Perez (*Avengers, Titans, Crisis on Infinite Earths*)

Bill Sienkiewicz (*New Mutants, Moon Knight, Dazzler*)

Getting the 411 on Comics

THERE IS A TON OF INFORMATION ABOUT COMIC BOOKS AVAILABLE. Where you look depends on what you want to learn. You can learn about the history of comic books, the artists and writers, the storylines, the prices, and more. You can use books, magazines, and Web sites to do your research.

For information about current issues, try the publishers' Web sites. They preview upcoming issues and story arcs. The previews include a plot summary and list the writers and artists who created the issue. The sites also **archive** information about past issues.

If you want to learn about the history of comics, go to the library. Many books have been written about Silver and Golden Age comic books and the people who created them.

To learn about the current value of comics, consult the *Overstreet Comic Book Price Guide*. It has prices for comic books from the Victorian Age through today. It also has many articles about the **market** for various titles.

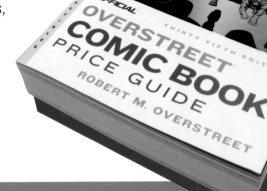

One thing you will notice right away when you look at pricing guides is the wide range of prices. Price depends on two main factors. The first is availability.

The rule of supply and demand says that when demand is high and supply is low, prices are high. Old comic books in good shape are in high demand. And, there aren't that many of them, so the price is high.

When demand is low and supply is high, price is low. There are lots of copies of modern comic books.

There isn't much demand for them, so the price is relatively low.

The other thing that affects price is the condition, or grade, of the comic book. Let's say you have two copies of the very first *Fantastic Four*. The copy in near mint condition is worth about $35,000. The copy in good condition is worth just under $1,000.

Grading Comics

Grade is how comic book dealers and buyers describe the condition of a comic book. There are 25 grades ranging from poor to gem mint. There is also a 10-point scale that corresponds to these grades. Mostly you will see just eight grade names, though. Here are some of the characteristics that define each of these grades.

Grade Definitions

Mint (MT)

A comic book in mint condition looks as good as the day it was printed. Its cover is flat and bright, with no wear marks. There are no tears, folds, or creases inside or out. The staples binding the book are original, centered on the spine, and rust free. You are unlikely to find a pre-1970 comic book in mint condition.

Near Mint (NM)

A near mint comic book looks almost new. The cover must show no signs of wear. Slight tears to the interior pages are acceptable. The spine is intact, with no splits or rolling. There should be no tears around the staples and almost no stress marks.

Very Fine (VF)

A very fine comic book looks as if it has been handled very carefully. Its cover may show some small signs of wear, but its ink is still bright. The pages inside might have minor tears. The **centerfold** is still secure. There might be very minor cover tears and stress marks around the staples.

Fine (FN)

A fine comic book shows a little wear but is still in above-average condition. There might be minor wear and creasing on the cover, and it might not be very glossy anymore. There might be a little rolling along the spine. There might be minor tears and stress marks along the staples. Inside, the pages may have browned some and the centerfold may be loose.

Very Good (VG)

A very good comic looks as if it has been well read but not mistreated. The cover might be loose but is still attached. The centerfold may have come free from one staple. While there may be moderate tears, creases, soil, and fading, the pages and cover have no major tears.

Good (GD)

Comic books in good condition show substantial wear. They are scuffed up and creased. The cover and centerfold may be detached but are still there. Despite the defects, the book is still entirely readable. Most reading copies are graded good.

Fair (FR)

Comic books in fair condition are often heavily worn. The cover and all pages are still there, but may be missing small pieces. The pages are browned and brittle. The corners are probably rounded and creased. The spine usually is rolled, and tears along the staples are typical.

Poor (PR)

Comic books in poor condition are damaged. They are dirty, scuffed, faded, and possibly water damaged. They are missing big chunks or even entire pages. The pages are very brittle. Although these comics are not collectible, people who restore comic books may want them.

Cover Grading Guide

Rounded corners

Crease

Rust

Stress marks

Faded color

Spine roll

Worn edge

Interior Grading Guide

Edge damage

Tear

Brown paper

Coupon cut out

Crease

Loose centerfold

Buying Comics

BELIEVE IT OR NOT, YOU USED TO BE ABLE TO BUY NEW COMIC BOOKS JUST ABOUT EVERYWHERE. They were at newsstands, corner stores, gas stations, even grocery stores. The comic books were distributed by companies that distributed magazines.

Comic Book Stores

In the 1970s, comic book publishers began direct distribution. Comic book stores had opened all around the country. So, the publishers cut out the magazine distributors and sold directly to comic book stores. Now these stores are almost the only places to go buy new comics. Many comic book stores also sell older comics.

There are many advantages to shopping at a comic book store. You can usually place an order ahead of time for the titles you want. Some stores have an in-store subscription service. With this, you're guaranteed you'll get a copy of every issue. But unlike a regular mail subscription, the comic book won't be damaged in the mail.

In addition, the people who work at comic book stores are often huge fans of comics. If you go when the store isn't busy, you can usually spend some time talking to the sales staff. They know about comics, so you can learn from them.

Wednesday is a big day for comic book stores. That's when the new issues arrive. If you want new issues, that's the day to shop!

Comic Book Content

There are comic books for every age group. Some comic book publishers use a rating system. The ratings show which comic books are appropriate for different age groups.

There is a little history behind the rating systems. In the early 1950s, some comic book content had become very violent. Many parents and educators decided that reading comic books wasn't good for kids. In some places they even burned comic books!

In response to public outcry and hearings in the U.S. Senate, the comic book industry created the Comics Code Authority. The CCA set strict rules for comic book content. By **self-policing**, the industry hoped to avoid government **censorship**.

Free Comic Books!

Since 2001, comic book stores around the country have held a yearly Free Comic Book Day. Anyone who goes to a participating comic book store on that day can get one or more free comic books!

Today, things have changed again. Many educators and parents find value in letting kids read comic books. Some schools even use them in the classroom for classes on creative writing and drawing.

But keep in mind that not all comic books are made for kids. Some are very violent. Show the comic books you want to read to a parent or other trusted adult.

Comicons

Comic book dealers and collectors alike call comic book conventions "comicons." Some are huge events, drawing people from all over the country. Some are even international. And if you're lucky, there are comicons where you live.

Local comicons range in size from small to large. They are often held at hotels and convention centers. Sometimes they are held at local shopping malls. Anyone can attend a comicon. The staff at your local comic store can tell you when and where local comicons will be held.

Dress Up!

Sometimes people who go to comicons dress as their favorite comic book characters. It can be very fun to see all the creative outfits. But you don't have to dress up if you don't want to!

Perhaps the most important part of attending a comicon is the planning. Make a list of the issues you are looking for. This is called a wants list. Write down the issue number, the grade you want, and the current value.

Decide ahead of time how much money you are willing to spend. Budget some of the money to buy items on your wants list. And set aside some money that you can use to buy things you didn't know you wanted until you saw them!

Comicons are another great place to learn more about comic books. If they aren't busy, dealers will answer your questions. They can tell you about the comics they have and what's special about them.

Most dealers sell both valuable comics and reading copies. Always be careful when handling a dealer's comic books. It's a good idea to ask permission before taking anything out of a sleeve.

Bigger comicons are often attended by celebrities, especially comic book writers and artists. It's perfectly all right to ask them for autographs. Sometimes they even set up tables just for that purpose.

Flea Markets

Collectors of all sorts go to flea markets. They're kind of like huge yard sales. You won't find comic books at every flea market, but you'll usually find a dealer or two with some comic books.

It is common to **haggle** at flea markets. If you see something you would like, ask the price. If the price seems high, ask if that is the best price the dealer can offer you. If you ask politely, dealers will often lower the price some.

Online Shopping

Even if you don't buy online, you can shop online. Looking at online comic book stores will give you an idea about the prices for the items you want to collect. You'll quickly learn which comic books are common and which ones are rare.

If you do decide to buy something online, always have an adult help you. An adult can help you decide if a Web site is a safe one to buy from. Read reviews about the seller. Read the return policy. Read what to do if the item you buy doesn't look as good in reality as it did online.

Be especially careful if you buy something in an online auction. It is very easy to get caught up in the excitement and competition. And it's very easy to pay too much for something as a result!

Ask a Parent

Before you buy or sell anything online, make sure you receive permission from a parent or a guardian. He or she can help you enter the necessary credit information.

Original Comic Art

IF YOU REALLY ENJOY COMIC BOOK ART, IT'S NICE TO HAVE A PIECE OF ORIGINAL ART. Comic books are usually stored in boxes for safekeeping. But you can frame a piece of original artwork and enjoy it every day.

Until recently, no one paid much attention to the original art created for comic books. It was tossed into storage, given away, or even destroyed. Then comic book collectors became interested in collecting this art.

As with comic books, older artwork is scarce and valuable. Art is available in various stages of completion. If you look around online and in shops, you'll see pencil and ink sketches as well as some finished color art.

Today, comic book artists own the art they make. After the comic books are completed, the art is returned to the artists. Make sure that any art you buy is original, not a print made from the original.

Action Figures

SOME COMIC BOOK FANS COLLECT ANYTHING THEY CAN FIND THAT RELATES TO THEIR FAVORITE COMIC BOOK CHARACTERS. And that includes action figures!

Action figures have been popular since the 1970s. You can find older superhero action figures at flea markets, garage sales, and antiques stores. You can also find them at toy conventions. Toy conventions are similar to comicons, but they're for toy collectors.

Toy collectors pay more for toys that are in mint shape and still in their original packaging. If you buy new toys, you can leave them in their original packaging if you like. That may make them more valuable in the future.

But there is no guarantee that any one toy will become valuable. So, if you want to take your action figures out of the packages, go right ahead. Collecting is supposed to be fun, after all!

Organization and Storage

As you have seen, comic books that are in good shape are worth more than those that are beat up. If you plan to store your comic books, you need to protect them.

Comic books should be stored somewhere that is dry, dark, and cool. Water, light, humidity, insects, and hot temperatures will destroy your collection.

Do not store comic books in a basement, garage, or attic. These places tend to be damp, which will ruin paper very quickly. If possible, store your comic books in a dark room that is air-conditioned and where air can circulate. That protects them from extreme heat, keeps them away from light, and keeps them dry.

If you must store comic books in a closet, choose an interior closet. Boxes stored against exterior walls are more likely to be damaged by moisture and mold.

Storage Supplies

To store comic books long-term, you need three items. These are boxes, backing boards, and sleeves. Before you buy any supplies, though, you need to know what size to buy.

Comic books have become narrower over time. The companies that make storage supplies make different sizes for each size of comic book.

Boxes

Comic books should be stored standing up. When they are stored flat, they can slide around. That scuffs the covers. It can also loosen the covers or contribute to spine roll.

Boxes for storing comic books come in long and short lengths. The long boxes usually hold about twice as many comic books as the short boxes. The boxes are strong and have lids, so you can stack them.

Look for boxes that are moisture resistant and insect resistant. But most important, look for boxes that are acid-free, or archival quality.

Box dividers are useful, especially if you store different series in one box. The dividers have tabs at the top that stick above the comic books. You can label the tabs to make it easier to find what you are looking for. Box dividers should also be acid-free.

Size It Up!

Golden Age comic books measure 7½ inches by 10½ inches.

Silver Age comic books measure 7 inches by 10½ inches.

Current comic books measure 6¾ inches by 10½ inches.

SLEEVES

Sleeves are special plastic bags for storing comic books. They protect the covers from tears, scuffs, and nicks. The best bags for long-term storage are Mylar. If you use polypropylene or polyethylene bags, be sure to change them every few years. These materials give off gas as they age and can damage comic books.

Thicker bags are more expensive, but last longer. Thickness of plastic is measured in mils. If you buy resealable bags, look for those with an adhesive strip on the bag, not the flap. Adhesive on the flap can stick to the comic book as you slide it in or out of the bag.

Be very careful when putting comic books into sleeves. It's easy to catch the cover on the edge of the bag, especially if the cover already has a small tear.

BACKING BOARDS

Backing boards add stiffness to the comic books. They keep the comic books from curling and protect the edges. Backing boards absorb some acid from the comic books. Be sure to replace backing boards every few years. Use only acid-free backings.

What Is Archival Quality?

Archival-quality products are free of the acids that can damage paper. They cost more, but will help your comic books last longer. Be sure that the boxes, backings, and sleeves you buy are archival quality.

29

Conclusion

LONGTIME COLLECTORS KNOW THAT THEIR INTEREST IN COLLECTING COMES AND GOES. After collecting avidly for years, they may lose interest. When this happens, they just leave their collection in a safe place and wait. Usually they become interested again.

This is very common with young collectors. People in their teens and twenties are busy with school and other duties. They often don't have time for their collections.

If this happens to you, that's okay. Collecting is for fun. If you are too busy to enjoy the time you spend on your hobby, just put it away. It will be there when you have time to enjoy it again!

Glossary

anthology – a collection of stories, essays, or poems.

archive – to collect and preserve documents and records.

censorship – having removed or suppressed material that is considered by some to be offensive.

centerfold – the sheet of paper that contains the center pages of a book or magazine.

Cold War – a period of tension and hostility between the United States and its allies and the Soviet Union and its allies after World War II.

continuity – the uninterrupted flow of storyline details from one episode to the next in a comic book, television, radio, or film series.

haggle – to bargain over the price of something.

market – a specific group of possible buyers.

self-police – to control or keep order of oneself.

sequential – following one after another in order.

World War II – a global conflict that ended in 1945.

Web Sites

To learn more about collecting comic books, visit ABDO Publishing on the World Wide Web at **www.abdopublishing.com**. Web sites about comic book collecting are featured on our Book Links page. These links are routinely monitored and updated to provide the most current information available.

Index